Jeff Tracy was an engineer and astronaut who decided to do something to help people in mortal danger. Having amassed a vast fortune in business, he spent his billions secretly constructing a fleet of five Thunderbirds - amazing machines invented by his friend Brains, the world's top scientific genius. Thus International Rescue came into being. From its base on a luxurious Pacific island, this secret organization is always ready to speed to the aid of anyone in peril.

Each craft is unique. Thunderbird One, piloted by Scott Tracy, can race to the scene of a disaster at nine times the speed of sound. Often it is followed by Thunderbird Two, manned by Virgil Tracy, which brings an array of special rescue machines aboard its equipment pod. When catastrophe looms in space, Alan Tracy rockets to the rescue in Thunderbird Three. And for undersea calamities, there is the versatile one-man submarine Thunderbird Four, operated by Gordon Tracy. Last but not least, Thunderbird Five, orbiting far up in space, is manned by John Tracy, constantly on the alert to pick up distress calls. Back on Earth, International Rescue receive vital help from their agent in England, Lady Penelope. Together with her butler, Parker, she maintains the strict secrecy that is essential for the successful operation of International Rescue.

No matter what the risk to themselves, and despite the opposition of master criminals like the Hood, Jeff and his sons have pledged to give their aid to anyone in danger. And so, when earthquakes, fires, crashes or explosions threaten human life, the signal goes out: 'Calling International Rescue . . .' and then THUNDERBIRDS ARE GO!

Also available in
the THUNDERBIRDS series,
and published by Young Corgi Books:

BRINK OF DISASTER

Forthcoming:
SUN PROBE
ATLANTIC INFERNO

THUNDERBIRDS: THE UNINVITED
A YOUNG CORGI BOOK 0 552 527637

First publication in Great Britain

PRINTING HISTORY
Young Corgi edition published 1992

Cover and inside artwork by Arkadia

This book is set in 14/18 pt Garamond 3 by
Phoenix Typesetting, Burley-in-Wharfedale, West Yorkshire

Young Corgi Books are published by
Transworld Publishers Ltd, 61-63 Uxbridge Road, Ealing, London W5 5SA, in Australia by Transworld Publishers (Australia) Pty. Ltd, 15-23 Helles Avenue, Moorebank, NSW 2170, and in New Zealand by Transworld Publishers (N.Z.) Ltd, 3 William Pickering Drive, Albany, Auckland.

Made and printed in Great Britain by
Cox & Wyman Ltd, Reading, Berks.

THE UNINVITED

Dave Morris

YOUNG CORGI

Chapter One
SNEAK ATTACK

Scott was on his way back to base in Thunderbird One. He had been called to the scene of a fire that had broken out at an oil rig. But by the time he had arrived, the local emergency services already had the fire under control. Scott didn't mind a false alarm every now and then. After radioing a report back to Jeff Tracy, he was content to put Thunderbird One on autopilot and just settle back to enjoy the ride home.

Suddenly there was a loud crackle of gunfire and a shell skimmed along Thunderbird One's hull. Scott snapped to attention; as he grabbed the controls, he noticed a trio of fighter planes closing in on him. They had strange Z-shaped markings that he did not recognize. They were closing fast, and they were trying to shoot Scott down!

Scott yanked at the controls and sent Thunderbird One into a steep climb. Below, one of the fighters peeled off and streaked in pursuit while the others spread out. The Thunderbird's jets roared as Scott steered his craft around. His pursuer could not turn as quickly and went speeding past, but now the others were climbing to intercept.

'Base from Thunderbird One,' Scott radioed urgently. 'I'm under attack from three unidentified aircraft. Taking evasive action . . .'

It was all he had time to say. Moments later

Thunderbird One shuddered and went into an uncontrolled dive. A high-velocity shell from one of the fighters had found its target, smashing the steering jets. Scott struggled with the controls, but the Thunderbird was picking up speed. He heard the ominous whine of screeching engines and the wind whipping past the hull.

'I'm hit! I'm going down over the Sahara—' he yelled into the radio. Below, he could see the vast dunes of the Sahara Desert rushing up towards him. At the last moment, he felt the Thunderbird beginning to respond. The nose began to rise, but it was too late to pull out of the dive. A crash-landing was the best he could hope for.

The impact as Thunderbird One hit the sand sent Scott flying. His head struck the control column and he was hardly conscious as the huge craft went ploughing

TB1

through the sand dunes. As it came to rest, the three fighter planes flew overhead to survey the damage. Their leader, satisfied that no-one could have survived the landing, ordered them to return to their hidden base and Thunderbird One was left silent and alone amid the dunes.

'Slow down, Wilson,' said Lindsay nervously. 'If you drive too fast on this sand you're liable to crash and kill us both!'

Wilson's response was to scowl and press down even harder on the accelerator. He and Lindsay were archaeologists. For fifteen days they'd been out in the desert, searching for a lost pyramid. The merciless scorching sun, dusty air, the uncomfortable shaking of the truck, and Lindsay's constant griping had left Wilson in a very bad mood. Now all he wanted to do was get back to civilization and enjoy a long ice-cold drink.

'Hey, look!' piped up Lindsay. 'What's that over there?'

Wilson sighed and turned to look. He couldn't see anything – apart, of course, from the endless expanse of sand dunes that lay in every direction. 'Nothing,' he grunted. 'A mirage, maybe. Or perhaps the sun's baked your brains so much that you're seeing things.'

But Lindsay was sure he'd seen something. It had looked like a glint of metal. Now it had passed behind the nearest dune, but as they drove on he kept straining his eyes in that direction. Then, as they passed the end of the dune, it came in sight again: a massive sky rocket. It lay at the end of a deep furrow in the sand, as if it had made a forced landing.

'You see?' cried Lindsay triumphantly. 'You call *that* a mirage?'

Wilson drove the truck over to take a

closer look. Now they could make out the designs painted on the tail. 'Wilson,' said Lindsay excitedly, 'I think it's International Rescue!'

Then they spotted an open hatchway in the side of the craft. A figure in a blue uniform was slumped across it. Wilson and Lindsay fetched the first-aid kit from the supply wagon towed behind their truck and hurried over.

Lindsay was horrified that the craft's pilot

might be dead, so he was very relieved when his eyes fluttered open. There was a nasty gash along his forehead, but other than that he seemed no worse than bruised.

'Must have blacked out . . .' groaned Scott, gingerly probing the cut. 'I remember opening the hatch, and that's all.'

'You're not too badly hurt,' Wilson replied. 'But we'd better clean that wound up and get a dressing on it.'

'Fine,' agreed Scott, 'but first maybe you'd do me a favour. Will you call International Rescue and let them know I'm OK? I'd do it myself, but I think my radio was smashed by the impact.'

Lindsay nodded. 'Sure. What radio frequency should I use?'

Scott smiled. 'Oh, I guess any frequency will do. We have some pretty sophisticated monitoring equipment, you know.'

* * *

Within a minute the call had been received aboard Thunderbird Five, high above in orbit around the Earth. John Tracy lost no time in relaying the glad tidings to his father and brothers at International Rescue headquarters.

'That's excellent news,' said Jeff Tracy, breathing a quiet sigh of relief. He hadn't wanted his sons to realize quite how worried he had become. Now he sent out a call to Virgil, who was already en route to the Sahara aboard Thunderbird Two along with Brains and Tin-Tin.

Once they pinpointed the exact co-ordinates, it was easy to locate the crashed Thunderbird. As Virgil touched down on the sand, Brains was already assembling the repair equipment he needed to make Thunderbird One airworthy once more.

While Brains worked into the evening, Tin-Tin prepared a meal and Scott and Virgil began talking to the two archaeologists. 'I don't know if those fighters will be around to try anything tomorrow,' Scott was saying. 'But if they are, they're going to find Thunderbirds aren't such easy targets when they're aware of a possible attack.'

'Who could they have been?' mused Lindsay. 'There's no airbase around here – there aren't people for hundreds of miles.'

Wilson stared at the camp-fire. 'There's something about this part of the desert,' he said, half to himself. 'It's like something eerie that you can't quite put your finger on. I've felt it all the time we've been looking for that pyramid.'

Virgil was intrigued. 'I've never heard of any pyramids this far into the desert.'

'It's the lost pyramid of Khamandides,' Lindsay explained. 'Over the years, several explorers claim to have caught sight of it – in sandstorms and so on – but no-one's ever actually found it. Some people believe it's real, and some just explain the sightings away as a mirage or a trick of the imagination.' He gave Wilson a resentful glance as he said this.

Tin-Tin could see that the two archaeologists' tempers were frayed from long isolation in the desert. 'Well, it's been a long day and we're all tired,' she said. 'I suggest we get some sleep.'

As they were bedding down for the night beside Thunderbird Two, on the other side of the world the sun was rising. Jeff Tracy had already been up and at his desk for several hours, using data from Thunderbird Five to try and discover who had piloted the planes that attacked Scott. He could find no evidence that they had come from any national air force. No flight plans had been logged, and in any case who would fly patrols right out over the middle of the desert? There was nothing worth protecting there.

Probably it had just been a misunderstanding, he told himself. The fighters might have drifted off course and mistaken Thunderbird One for a missile. He shrugged and closed the file on the event. After all, Scott had been found safe and sound, and Brains had repaired Thunderbird One. It didn't matter now.

Chapter Two
DISASTER IN THE DESERT

Thick stinging clouds of sand shot up from the truck's wheels and the sunlight formed a harsh haze as far as the eye could see. It was the next morning and, after watching the Thunderbirds take off, Wilson and Lindsay were continuing their journey.

'Well, that was an adventure,' said Lindsay. 'And it made a nice change to see some new faces . . .'

'Yeah, yeah,' grunted Wilson irritably, 'I know what you're getting at. Don't think I'm not sick of your ugly mug, too. I just wish we could've had as much luck finding the pyramid as we did stumbling across that Thunderbird.'

Lindsay mopped a trickle of sweat from his brow. His throat was dry and his mouth tasted of grit, but he didn't want to reach for the water-can because he knew it would just provoke Wilson into snapping at him. Wilson always kept a sharp eye on their water rations, and he laid down the rules like a tyrant. If only Wilson were such a stickler for other rules, thought Lindsay . . . like now, he was driving much too fast again.

'Why don't you let me take a spell at the wheel?' Lindsay suggested.

Wilson gave a snort of derision. 'Sure, and take another two weeks to get home? No thanks.' He shifted gear to get the truck up a steep dune.

Over the roar of the engine, neither of them noticed a warning creak of stressed metal from the back of the truck.

'We're sliding all over the place,' said Lindsay as the tyres fought for a hold in the sand. 'Slow down, for goodness' sake!'

'Will you quit complaining?' Wilson snarled as they reached the top of the dune and started down the other side. 'I've been doing most of the driving on this trip and we haven't crashed, have we?'

If Wilson hadn't been yelling, they might have heard a shriek of breaking metal. The pin holding the supply trailer to the back of the truck was beginning to give way.

Suddenly Wilson felt the truck starting to skid to one side. Hurriedly he jerked the wheel around, but the extra strain was more than the fatigued metal could bear. The trailer broke free and went tumbling down to land in a shattered ruin at the bottom of the slope.

Wilson brought the truck to a halt. 'Whew! That was a close call.'

'I told you,' Lindsay said angrily. 'Now we'll have to go down and unpack the essential supplies. All our water and food are on that trailer – '

He was cut off by the sound of an explosion from the bottom of the slope. Before their horrified eyes, a plume of flame rose from the trailer, wreathed in thick black petroleum smoke.

'. . . And our gasoline,' groaned Wilson. Obviously a spark had ignited it, blasting all their vital supplies to smithereens. They were stranded in the Sahara, five hundred kilometres from their base camp, with only three gallons of petrol left in the tank. Enough

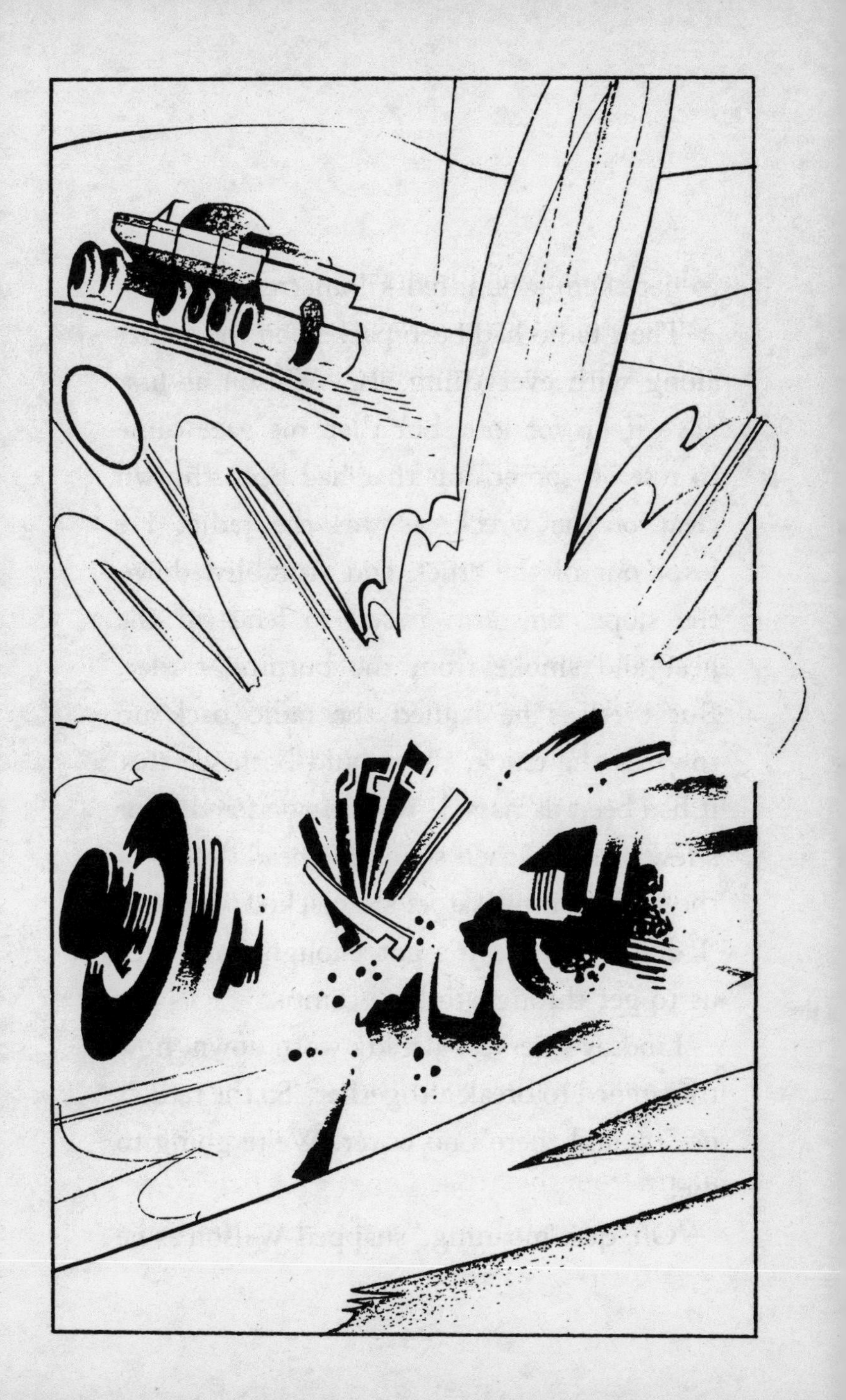

to get them a hundred kilometres at best.

Their radio had been packed on the trailer along with everything else. Wilson at first gave it up for lost, but then his gaze came to rest on something that had been thrown clear of the wreck. It was the radio! He leapt out of the truck and stumbled down the slope, one arm raised to fend off the heat and smoke from the burning trailer. But even as he hauled the radio back up towards the truck, they could both see that it had been damaged. Wilson pondered it for a few seconds, then shook his head. 'Most of the wave compensators are cracked,' he said. 'I don't suppose it's got enough power for us to get through to base camp.'

Lindsay's nerves, already worn down, now threatened to break altogether. 'So the radio's useless and there's no water. We're going to die!'

'Oh, quit moaning,' snapped Wilson as he

hoisted the radio into the truck. 'Maybe we can get this thing fixed. In the meantime, we've got enough petrol to take us maybe a hundred kilometres. Which way do you want to go?'

Lindsay stared up into the sky, where the sun met his hopeless gaze with its own relentless glare. 'That's a stupid question,' he moaned as he wiped the sand-caked sweat off his face. 'Whichever way we go, always there's just sand and more sand . . .'

Wilson was studying a map. Suddenly he tossed it into the truck and jumped back in behind the wheel. 'Yes,' he said with an excited note in his voice. 'But they have waterholes in the desert and I just spotted one on the map. It's only eighty kilometres due north of here.'

'We might just make it,' said Lindsay with renewed hope as Wilson revved the engine.

Wilson nodded. 'But just in case something goes wrong, you'd better keep trying the radio. The signal's faint, but there's a chance someone will hear us.'

At about the same time, Scott and Alan were getting ready for a trip. This was no ordinary trip, though: Scott was taking Alan up to Thunderbird Five so that their brother John could come down to Earth for a well-earned rest. It meant that Scott would have to pilot Thunderbird Three, but that did not worry him. Each of the Tracy brothers was trained to operate any of the Thunderbirds if the need arose.

'OK,' said Jeff Tracy, glancing at his watch. 'You two had better be on your way. John's probably already packed his bags.'

He touched a button on his desk and the couch on which Scott and Alan were sitting sank into the floor. As they were lowered down an underground shaft, a duplicate couch rose into position above them.

Reaching the bottom of the shaft, the couch trundled along a tunnel and into the huge hangar where Thunderbird Three rested on its launch pad. There was a whine of hydraulic pistons and Scott and Alan were swiftly raised up into the body of the gleaming spaceship.

Within minutes they were ready for lift-off. Amid a mighty roar of powerful rockets, Thunderbird Three soared up into the sky and soon it could only be seen as a distant red point atop the white flare of its thrusters.

Far up in space, John watched the approach of Thunderbird Three through the thick glass of a viewing port. He had been on duty in Thunderbird Five for over three months now, and he would be glad to get back down to Tracy Island. John was the most solitary of the Tracy brothers, but there

came a point where even he longed for some company and the chance to laze on the beach for a few days.

Scott's voice crackled over the radio: 'Thunderbird Three to space station. We are now docking. Prepare boarding tube.'

With expert precision, Scott brought Thunderbird Three alongside and then carefully steered the nose section into the docking bay. Magnetic locks formed an airtight seal to keep out the vacuum of space, and then the boarding tube slid into position against the rocket's hull.

Alan grabbed his bag and waved as he strode off down the boarding tube. 'So long, Scott. See you in a month's time.'

John looked up with a cheery smile as his brother walked on to the bridge of the space station. 'Hi, Alan,' he said. 'Well, it's all yours for the next four weeks. I hope you brought a couple of books to while away the time.'

Alan chuckled. 'Oh, I'm sure I'll find plenty to keep me busy. Anything I should be watching out for in particular?'

'Hmm, I'm not really sure,' John answered. 'I did think I picked up something from the Sahara region just as you were docking. It was a very faint signal, and then it stopped.'

'Probably nothing,' said Alan, 'but I'll keep my ears open just in case. Bye, then, John; enjoy your holiday.'

* * *

The needle on the petrol gauge was flickering close to empty by the time Wilson and Lindsay caught sight of the oasis. When Lindsay saw the tall palm trees along the horizon, he gave a whoop of joy and grabbed hold of Wilson's arm. 'Look, it's the waterhole! We're saved!' he cried.

'Let go of my arm, for Pete's sake,' grumbled Wilson. 'You'll make me crash the truck.'

Lindsay scowled at him. 'Too bad you weren't such a cautious driver earlier on,' was all he said for the rest of the drive.

They felt their mouths watering as the swaying green fronds of the oasis came closer through the dust haze. But then Wilson saw something and he eased his foot off the pedal, muttering curses under his breath as he did.

'What's wrong?' said Lindsay urgently. 'Don't slow down now; I can't wait to get a taste of that water.'

'Just look at that waterhole,' said Lindsay, shaking his head. 'The only taste you'll get from that is grit.'

It was true. The oasis was dry!

Chapter Three
THE LOST PYRAMID

'Calling International Rescue. Come in please. We are stranded . . . need water . . . come in, International Rescue . . .'

Alan switched off the tape playback. 'That call came in just a few minutes ago, Father,' he explained. 'It was the same waveband as an earlier signal that John told me about.'

In his study on Tracy Island, Jeff was facing the row of portraits of his sons.

For the time being, the portrait of Alan was replaced by a TV screen showing Alan himself, high above in Thunderbird Five.

'Where was it broadcast from?' asked Jeff.

Alan shook his head. 'I don't know, Father. It was somewhere in the Sahara region, but I can't tell exactly. It was very faint, and then it faded out altogether.'

The walls of the study vibrated as the sound of a rocket landing thundered from outside. It was Thunderbird Three returning to base. That gave Jeff an idea. He asked Alan to wait until Scott came up from the hangar, and then to play the message back again.

Scott recognized the voice at once. 'That's Wilson – one of the archaeologists who saved me,' he said.

'I thought as much,' said Jeff. 'Well, one good turn deserves another. Fly out to the Sahara and see if you can find them, Scott.

And be sure to go at top speed; when a man's stuck without water in the desert, things can get desperate rather quickly!'

Wilson took off the headset and flung the radio out of the truck in disgust. 'It finally packed up,' he said. 'I couldn't tell if I got through to International Rescue or not. But I guess that was our last hope.'

Lindsay had begun to shiver. He wasn't cold, of course; he was starting to panic. Then he saw something, far away on the horizon. It was just a faint blur in the heat haze, but it made Lindsay forget all about his troubles. 'Look there,' he cried, clutching Wilson's arm. 'It's the pyramid!'

Wilson peered out across the desert. All he could see was the blistering haze of wind-blown sand. 'Another mirage,' he grunted.

'No,' insisted Lindsay. 'Over there.'

The wind dropped, and as it did the haze

dropped away like a curtain of lace. Shimmering like gold in the desert sun, they could both now see an unmistakeable triangular shape in the distance beyond the dunes.

'Holy smoke,' exclaimed Wilson. 'We've found it.'

Lindsay nodded. 'Yes, it's what we've been looking for all this time. The lost pyramid of Khamandides!'

Wilson glanced at the fuel gauge. They had just about enough petrol left to reach the pyramid. Immediately he started the ignition and began to steer the truck around.

'What's the use now? We'll be dead of heat exhaustion within a couple of hours,' said Lindsay. He was succumbing to despair again.

Wilson was made of sterner stuff. 'There's always a chance,' he said as he drove the truck out under the dusty palms of the dried-up oasis. 'There might be a nomad tribe camped near it. And they'd have water!'

The truck rumbled across the dunes, drawing agonizingly closer to the mysterious pyramid. Lindsay kept staring at the fuel gauge. It was dropping lower and lower, but he was silently praying that there was enough petrol left. This really was their last hope.

'It's magnificent,' Lindsay gasped as they arrived at the pyramid. They had no sooner driven into its shadow than the engine sputtered and died.

They both looked up at the pyramid – a huge man-made mountain of stone looming against the hot blue sky. It was the biggest of its kind that either of them had ever seen. Strange carvings covered the masonry blocks around its base. They were hieroglyphs, the language of the ancient Egyptians. But, imposing though the sight was, it only filled them with despair, because now they could see that the place was deserted.

Wilson's shirt was sticking to his back, soaked in sweat, and he was weak with heatstroke. Wearily he climbed out of the truck and staggered over to lean against the pyramid. Each block of stone was bigger than a man, and the sun had baked them all day until they were almost too hot to touch. 'So much for that nomad tribe we were counting on,' he muttered.

'Look at these hieroglyphs,' said Lindsay as he stumbled over. 'I can read some of them:

"This is the tomb of King Khamandides . . . God of the Eternal Fountain".'

Wilson managed a weak laugh. 'Eternal Fountain, my foot! I guess it ran dry.' He thought the inscription referred to the oasis they had passed through.

They were both startled by a grating sound. As Lindsay had stepped up to the inscription, the block of stone it was written on had suddenly begun to slide up, revealing an entrance into the pyramid. A cool gust of air wafted out. There was no time to gaze in amazement, because then they heard a faint sound that filled them with fresh hope. It was the trickle of water, and it came from somewhere inside the pyramid.

'How did the door open?' said Lindsay.

Wilson strode forward into the darkened entrance. 'Who cares? Come on – let's find that water.'

They stepped through to be confronted

with an awesome sight. Huge statues of long-dead Egyptian warriors lined the walls of the entrance chamber. Wilson snapped on his pocket torch and it shone on a sparkling mosaic of gold and rich blue.

The sound of running water was louder now. Enticed by it, they stepped further across the room. But they should have been more cautious, because suddenly the stone block slid back into place across the entrance, sealing them in.

They spun round as they heard the block settle into place. Lindsay felt a twinge of rising terror. 'We're trapped!' he wailed.

'Surely there'll be a way to open the door from inside,' said Wilson. He wished he was as confident as he tried to sound. The ancient Egyptians had built many traps into their pyramids to deal with would-be tomb robbers.

Lindsay started to feel along the walls.

His boot caught on something that gave a brittle snap as his weight rested on it. Wilson shone his torch down and there, on the floor beside the sealed exit, they saw something they had failed to notice before. It was a human skeleton.

'Looks like there's no escape,' said Wilson. 'This poor devil must have stumbled in here years ago. He looked for a way to open the door, but never found it.'

Lindsay wanted to scream. 'What do we do now?' he sobbed.

Wilson shrugged and headed off deeper into the pyramid. He had always been a practical sort of man. 'I don't know about you, but I'm going to find that water.'

A short corridor led them to another chamber at the bottom of a short flight of steps. This was where the sound was coming from. In the centre of the floor, sparkling deliciously in the light of the torch, they saw an ornate fountain bubbling over with water. It was the Eternal Fountain that the carvings outside had mentioned. Abandoning all dignity, they rushed over and plunged their heads into it. It was gloriously cool and sweet, and both drank deeply in spite of the pain in their parched throats.

'Mmm,' said Lindsay at last. 'I've never had a more refreshing drink.'

'And look at this,' said Wilson. He was playing the beam of his torch across the rear wall. It revealed a massive pile of golden artifacts: plates, statuettes and ornaments that glittered with a thousand precious jewels.

Lindsay gave vent to a nervous laugh. 'We're rich,' he giggled. 'We're the richest men in the world!'

All thought of their predicament had vanished for the moment. Both men lifted up great armfuls of treasure and flung them delightedly up in the air. 'We'll go down in history, Lindsay!' said Wilson. 'We'll be famous as the discoverers of the lost treasure of Khamandides.'

A polite cough made them both spin round, gold glistening in their hands and strange guilty expressions on their faces.

Scott Tracy was standing at the top of the steps. 'Hello again,' he said. 'I spotted your abandoned truck from the air and then found the entrance. It seems to have shut behind us, but I'll radio my brother to come and get us out . . .' In his hand was a communicator. He raised it to his lips and said: 'Virgil, this is Scott – '

The crack of a gunshot echoed across the chamber. Scott felt the communicator wrenched from his hand and saw it rebound, broken, off the stone wall. His hand stung from where the bullet had grazed him, but he hardly noticed the pain. He was rooted to the spot, staring in surprise and disbelief at the gun in Lindsay's hand.

'Lindsay, you idiot!' shouted Wilson. 'What did you shoot at him for? He's come to rescue us.'

Lindsay's nerve-wracking experiences had finally snapped his sanity. 'No he hasn't,' he snarled. 'He's come to steal the treasure. *My* treasure!'

Wilson barely had time to dive to one side as Lindsay shot again – this time at him. The bullet sent splinters of stone hurtling from the wall.

The distraction gave Scott time to recover enough from his astonishment and take cover. Seeing two tall statues on each side of the doorway, he dived behind one of them. It was not a moment too soon. Lindsay had whirled back and now had the gun levelled at him again. Scott reached for his own gun, though he desperately wished he wouldn't have to use it. International Rescue's mission was to save people, not shoot them. But how was he going to save someone who didn't want to be saved?

'Come on, Lindsay,' he coaxed, 'put down that gun. You've been through a tough time. You need medical help.'

'Sure I do,' said Lindsay sarcastically. 'Then you'd be able to get my treasure, wouldn't you?' He fired again, the bullet chipping the statue Scott was using for cover.

Scott realized he was going to have to shoot it out. He took a couple of shots over Lindsay's head, hoping to shock him into giving up. Lindsay was convinced, though, that Scott and Wilson were after the treasure all for themselves. He began firing wildly, and his next bullet scored a lucky hit on Scott's gun and tore it out of the Thunderbird pilot's grasp. Scott watched aghast as the

gun clattered down the steps and landed at Lindsay's feet.

Lindsay snatched up the gun. Now he had two weapons. Gunshots rattled off the statue in rapid succession, each shattering a chunk of stone into dust and rubble. Within moments Scott's cover was blasted away and he stood defenceless against Lindsay's next shot.

'There's nowhere to hide, Tracy,' cackled Lindsay. 'Now you're going to die!'

Scott closed his eyes. A shot rang out –

Amazingly, Scott found he was still alive. He opened his eyes to see why. He was amazed to see that a section of the wall had suddenly slid open behind Lindsay and two strange men were standing in the secret passage there. The men were foreign-looking, with bizarre metal clothing emblazoned with a letter Z. One of the men had a gun, and from the wisp of smoke curling up from it

Scott guessed that this was the source of the shot he'd heard. The man had shot Lindsay's gun out of his hand a split second before the crazed archaeologist had time to shoot Scott.

'Thanks – ' began Scott.

But the stranger cut him off with a stream of harsh language. None of them recognized the words, but the meaning was obvious from the man's expression and the way he waved his gun. Scott and the others were his prisoners . . .

Chapter Four
CAPTIVES OF THE ZOMBITES

Jeff Tracy realized something was wrong the moment he lost contact with Scott.

'I don't like it,' he said. 'The radio went dead in mid-message. Virgil, you and Gordon take Thunderbird Two and get out to that pyramid as quickly as you can. International Rescue is depending on you now.'

In no time, Thunderbird Two was streaking westwards through the clouds. Virgil calculated it would take about eighty minutes to reach the Sahara Desert. That was a good time – one which no commercial aircraft could match, second only to Thunderbird One's speed. But it did not stop Virgil from worrying about his brother. There was no telling what kind of trouble Scott was in, and a lot could happen in eighty minutes.

Virgil opened up a radio channel. 'We're under way, Father,' he reported. 'I just hope we get there in time.'

'So do we all, Virgil,' came Jeff's solemn reply.

Meanwhile, Scott and the others had been forced at gunpoint into a monorail car that conveyed them slowly across the roof of a colossal underground chamber. It was bigger than all the Thunderbird hangars put together. Lindsay and Wilson were astounded to see something modern like this beneath a pyramid that was several thousand years old. They could only gape down through the monorail car window at the teeming activity below them. From up there, the mysterious Zombite workers looked like so many ants, bustling to and fro as they supervised the fuelling of a fleet of jet planes.

For Scott it was as though the last pieces of a jigsaw were fitting into place. 'Those look like the planes that shot me down,' he murmured. 'But who are these jokers?'

Lindsay had begun to recover from his brief spell of madness. He shook his head as though dazed and said, 'Perhaps they're some kind of lost race, living down here in the bowels of the earth, hidden from the modern world.'

Despite the danger of the situation, Wilson had retained his usual sense of curiosity. 'See those?' he said, pointing to a network of industrial pipes and pressure tanks on the chamber floor. 'It looks as though they've discovered an ore which gives off a highly explosive gas. That must be the source of their power.'

'Not just explosive, but poisonous too,' said Scott. He had noticed how the Zombite workers were all wearing gas masks. There were even stray fumes of the gas drifting around the monorail car. If it were not for the sealed glass windows, they would have been choking.

The monorail car reached the far end of the chamber and a shutter opened to let it pass through. They glided to a halt in a control room that overlooked the hangar. Zombites sat at various computer consoles, obviously keeping a close watch on the pressure in the gas pipes. Scott had seen enough disasters in his time to know that every power plant needed constant vigilance. There was always the danger of an accident that could blow such a place sky high.

Here in the control room there were no gas fumes, and the door of the car opened so that one of their guards could step out. He approached a Zombite who appeared to be the leader and spoke in his strange language. It looked as though he was telling the leader about his three captives.

The leader was too busy to be bothered with such distractions for the time being. He snapped back a few harsh words and pointed to a viewing screen on one wall of the control room. Scott turned to see what he was excited about and gave a gasp. The screen showed Thunderbird Two flying towards the desert. The leader touched a button on the console beside him and a luminous

framework appeared on the screen. As he pushed a control lever, the framework moved across and locked in position over Thunderbird Two. Scott could also see a battery of missiles rising into firing position beneath a rocket tube leading to the surface . . .

'They mean to shoot down Thunderbird Two,' Scott cried. 'We've got to warn Virgil!'

Wilson had been in a few brawls, and he knew what to do without being told twice.

There was now only one armed guard in the monorail car with them. Wilson turned, grabbed the guard's arm, and drove his knuckles into the tendons of his wrist. The guard gave a yelp – as much out of surprise as out of pain – and let go of the gun. Wilson tackled him, sending the two of them tumbling over towards the back of the car.

Scott moved fast. Seizing the fallen gun, he fired a random shot into the control room. The bullet hit one of the Zombite technicians, who collapsed across the control panel. His head struck the control lever just as the Zombite leader gave the order to fire. There was a roar of rockets from the hangar as the missiles launched, thundering up the rocket tubes and into the sky. If not for Scott's prompt action, Thunderbird Two would have been destroyed. As it was, the missiles sped past several metres wide of the mark and flew off to explode harmlessly somewhere above the desert.

Scott took the time for a couple more shots, aiming more carefully now. He was satisfied to see a fizzing shower of sparks issue from the computer consoles. Panic broke out in the control room as technicians fell over each other in their haste to grab fire extinguishers.

Only the Zombite leader stayed calm. He fixed Scott with a poisonous look of hatred and pressed a button on his control panel. A siren started blaring out across the underground complex.

'That will bring more guards,' Scott realized. 'Lindsay, get over to the controls. See if you can get this car moving.'

But Lindsay just stood and stared. He was frozen with fear. Fortunately, it was just then that Wilson managed to begin winning his struggle with the Zombite guard. Knocking the man out with a powerful punch to the jaw, he lost no time in leaping behind the controls and starting the car. With frightening slowness, the monorail car inched out of its parking bay and started on the long journey back across the hangar roof.

'Can't you get this thing to go any faster?' Scott asked Wilson.

'Sorry,' replied the archaeologist. 'This is maximum speed now.'

'Then maybe it's time to spread a bit more mayhem to cover our escape,' said Scott. Inching open the monorail door while keeping one hand over his face to avoid the gas fumes, he fired several shots down at the pressure tanks below. The Zombite workers screamed and ran as one of the shots split open a fuel line, releasing billows of lethal gas into the air.

Soon Scott could hardly see the floor of the chamber under a thick cloud of gas. The deadly white fumes drifted up to the monorail car, and he hastily pulled the door shut. The three men could hear muffled explosions from below as sparks from the short-circuiting computers caused pockets of gas to ignite.

'What's going on?' asked Lindsay.

Scott set his jaw grimly. 'The pressure in those fuel pipes has gone out of control,' he said. 'Unless I'm mistaken, this whole place is going to blow up.'

'I hope we're safely away before it does,' Wilson remarked dryly.

'So do I,' said Scott. He was not thinking just of himself and the archaeologists. He knew that Virgil would be coming in to land in Thunderbird Two by now. When the Zombites' underground lair went up, it would be with the force of a small atom bomb. Having lost his communicator, Scott had only his wristwatch radio to warn Virgil to get clear. And that would only work once he was outside the pyramid and into the open.

After what seemed like forever, the monorail car reached its other parking bay in the secret passage behind the Eternal Fountain. As the three men raced towards the exit, another thought sent a chill through them: 'What about the door?' said Lindsay. 'We couldn't get it open before!'

Luckily for them, the damage done to the Zombite computers by Scott's bullets had caused the control systems to fail. They found the door locked in a half-open position.

Scott dived through and sprawled in the sand. A shadow passed over him as Thunderbird Two glided into position beside the pyramid, its landing jets already firing for descent.

Scott flicked on his wristwatch radio. 'Virgil,' he said. 'Regain altitude and get clear. Quickly – the pyramid's about to explode!'

'But, Scott,' came back Virgil's voice, 'what about you?'

This was no time to argue. 'Just do as I say!' barked Scott. 'Go!'

Virgil did not need telling twice. Scott and the others saw the great bulk of Thunderbird Two rising higher into the sky as they ran towards Thunderbird One. Even through the sand and rock under their feet, they could feel the explosions rumbling up from deep beneath the ground. *Just a few seconds more . . .* Scott prayed silently to himself. *Dad would be really angry with me if I let myself get blown up. Not to mention Thunderbird One.*

Scott had never made the climb to Thunderbird One's flight deck as quickly. Jumping into the control chair, he began to fire up the boosters while Lindsay and Wilson were still climbing aboard. The Thunderbird lifted off and Scott fingered the main thruster control as they gained height.

'I'm going to give her everything she's got the moment the nose is clear of the top of the pyramid,' Scott told Virgil over the radio.

Virgil was watching with Gordon from the cabin of Thunderbird Two. 'But,' he replied, 'that will take you directly over the pyramid! What if it blows up just then?'

'No choice, I'm afraid,' said Scott. 'If I take the time to swing her around, we'd be blown to pieces for sure.' He turned to Lindsay and Wilson: 'Brace yourselves, you two. Thunderbird One can reach 10,000 kilometres an hour in just under one minute. That's a lot of acceleration!'

There was an ominous rumble from beneath them. Scott could not delay any

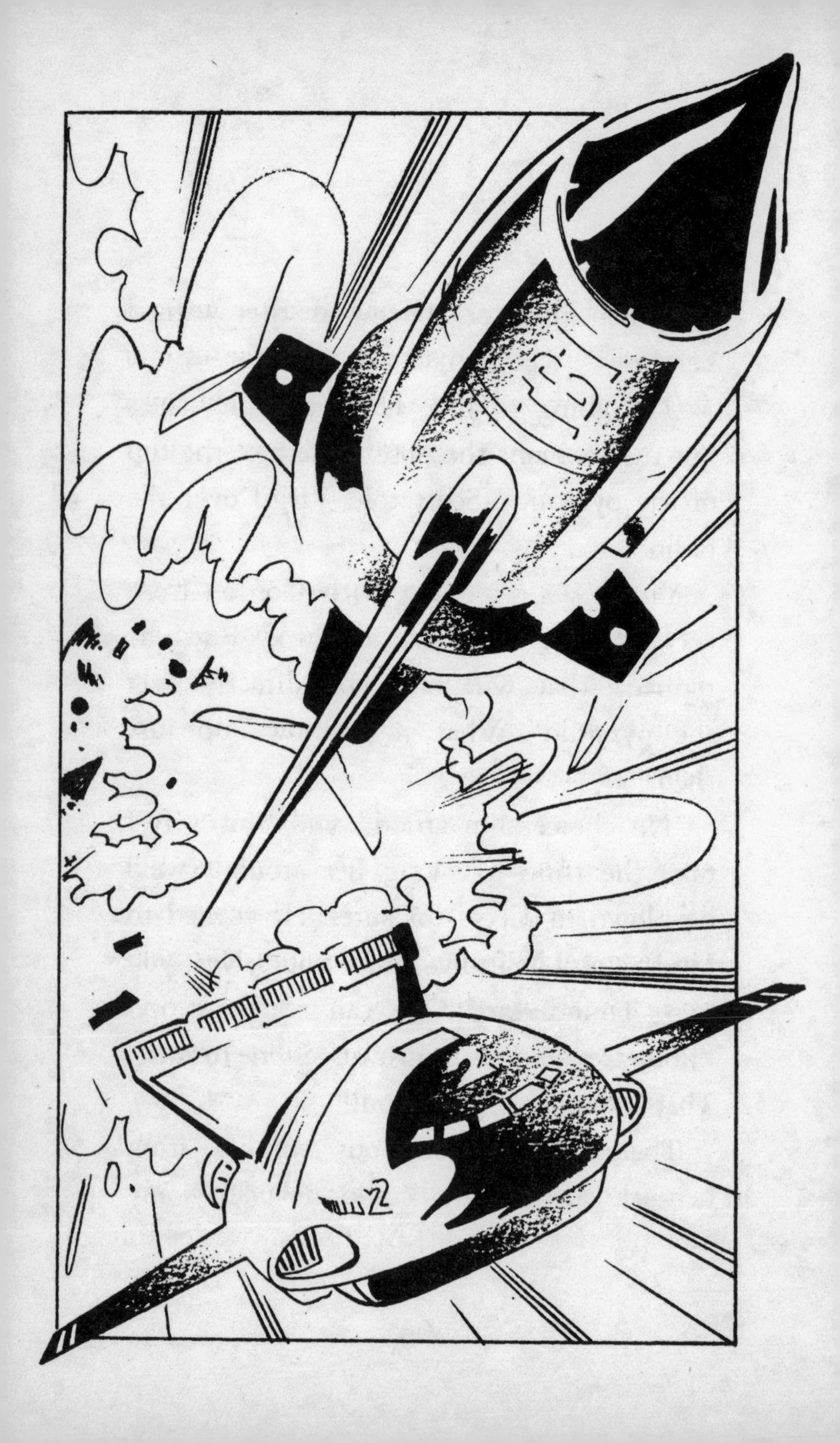

longer. He ignited the main booster and was pressed back into his chair with the instant G-force as Thunderbird One went roaring over the pyramid and up towards the cloudless blue sky.

It was not a moment too soon. As they watched, the build-up of gas finally caught in a chain reaction. The pyramid was blasted apart, massive chunks of rock hurtling like pebbles as a blinding fireball shot upwards from beneath it.

The two Thunderbirds circled the site once, in case there were any survivors. But all they could see was a deep chasm where the pyramid had stood, belching black smoke and cinders into the sky.

'So, it looks as though the lost pyramid of Khamandides is lost forever now,' said Scott.

Lindsay could only stare down at the smouldering ruin. 'Just think, we could have been in there when it blew up . . .' he said. 'We're lucky to have got away with our lives.'

'Yeah,' agreed Wilson. 'Thanks to International Rescue!'

THE END